GREAT WOLF
and the
GOOD WOODSMAN

written by Helen Hoover

illustrated by Charles Mikolaycak

Parents' Magazine Press: New York

OTHER BOOKS BY HELEN HOOVER

For adults

The Long-Shadowed Forest
The Gift of the Deer

For children

Animals at my Doorstep

Text Copyright © 1967 by Helen Hoover
Illustrations Copyright © 1967 by Charles Mikolaycak
Printed in the United States of America
Library of Congress Catalog Card Number 67-18463

To my husband, Adrian

Once, long years ago, Great Wolf stood on a high ridge and looked down at a deer, a squirrel and a chickadee, gathered together beside the log cabin where lived the Good Woodsman.
It was Christmas, and Great Wolf was very lonely. He was a mighty hunter, fleet of foot and sharp of tooth, and so he was feared by all the animals in the forest.

"Why doesn't the Good Woodsman come out?" the gentle deer was asking. "He always has fresh cedar branches for me to eat."
"And corn for me," chattered the squirrel.
"And seeds for me," the chickadee chirped, darting into the air. "I think something is wrong."

The squirrel scampered up the logs
to peer in the window, and gave
a startled squeak. The deer flashed
to his side, and the chickadee
flew up to the windowsill. Great Wolf
moved down the slope to a place
where he, too, could see inside,
and he saw the Good Woodsman,
sitting on the floor
holding his ankle.

"He's hurt," said the squirrel.
"He can't walk, and he will freeze without a fire. He has no coat like ours to keep him warm. We must get help!"
"There is a kind man in the house beside the lake," said the deer.
"I can run there— "
"And I can fly," added the chickadee.
"And I can chatter," said the squirrel. "But the man will not understand us. How can we make the man come with us?"

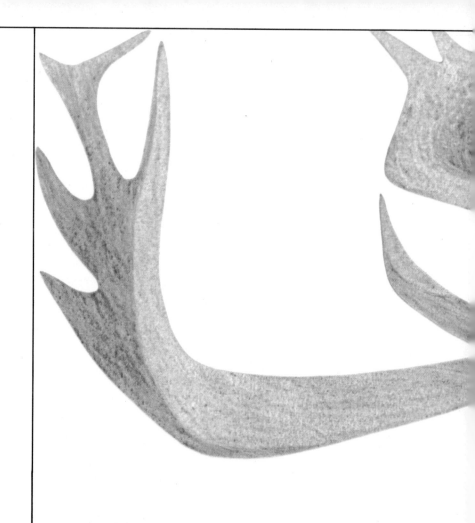

Great Wolf straightened up
and lifted his head, proud in the
knowledge that on this Christmas
Day he could offer a special gift
to his friend, the Good Woodsman.
While the other animals stood in an
anxious group, he walked slowly
and silently into the clearing.
"I can help you," he said as softly
as he could.

The squirrel jumped onto the roof,
and the deer in her fear and excite-
ment floundered in the deep snow.
Bravely, the little chickadee
flew around Great Wolf's head,
trying to frighten him away.

"Please don't be afraid," Great
Wolf said. "Don't you know
that on Christmas Day all animals
are friends? The Good Woodsman
has been kind to me as well as to
you, and now I can help him. I will
run over the hills to the house
of the man who lives beside the lake.
"The man is my enemy, but he has
a dog—and the dog and I are
cousins. I will tell the dog about
the Good Woodsman, and he can make
his master understand." And before
the animals could say a word, Great
Wolf leaped away, his gray fur
bright as silver in the sun, and his
green eyes shining.

When he came to the house beside the lake, he saw the man chopping wood. Great Wolf hesitated, for he feared the man. But there was no time for waiting. Leaping nimbly over the gleaming ice, straight past the man he ran, toward the house where lived his cousin, the dog.

"A wolf!" cried the man. He dropped his ax and ran for his rifle. But by that time Great Wolf had already told the dog about the Good Woodsman's accident, and was safely out of sight in the shadows under the trees.

The dog caught his master's pants
leg in his teeth and pulled toward
the path. Then he ran ahead and
waited. When the man hesitated, the
dog ran back to him and barked
eagerly. "You want me to come with
you, don't you?" the man said,
turning toward his house. He came
back wearing a fur-lined coat,
and followed the dog along the path,
while Great Wolf kept pace with
them through the forest.

Great Wolf hurried ahead and stood on the slope, watching and listening. The deer and the squirrel slipped into the shadows when they heard the man and the dog coming near, and the chickadee flew again to the windowsill. The dog barked at the Good Woodsman's door until the man opened it.

"What happened?" the man asked,
helping the Good Woodsman
to a chair.
"I stumbled over a piece
of stovewood and twisted my ankle.
It is lucky that you came by, for my
fire is out and I would have surely
frozen."
"It wasn't just luck,"
the man explained. "My dog brought
me here."
"Strange," said the Good
Woodsman. "I haven't seen him for
several days." Then he smiled.
"Perhaps one of my friends told him."

"Don't tell me your animals can talk," the man said laughing as he bandaged the Good Woodsman's ankle. "Not to you, but I think your dog can understand them—at least one of them," the Good Woodsman answered. He slowly stood up and leaned on the crutch the man had made from a bent stick. "I'll be fine now, thanks." He patted the dog. "And thank you, too!" The dog thumped his tail joyfully on the floor and barked his own special *Merry Christmas* to the Good Woodsman.

The Good Woodsman busied himself, hobbling about the cabin with his crutch. At last he opened the cabin door, carrying a Christmas feast of cedar and corn and seeds. The deer and the squirrel came out of the forest, and the chickadee flew down from the windowsill into a snow-drift. The Good Woodsman stood in the doorway watching his friends eat. Great Wolf, looking down from the ridge, was filled with a great gladness for them, but as he watched he grew lonelier than ever. "It is sometimes sad to be a mighty hunter, feared by all the animals," he said to himself.

Then the Good Woodsman brought out a plate of meat. "Come down, Great Wolf," he called. "Come down and have dinner with us."

Slowly Great Wolf stepped from
the shadows. "Welcome, Great Wolf,"
whispered the deer, trembling in
spite of herself.
"If it hadn't been for you,"
the squirrel said,
"this might have been a very sad
Christmas instead of a happy one."
And the chickadee perched on
Great Wolf's head to sing his little
song of gratitude.
"It is a very happy day for me,"
Great Wolf told
them, "for I have never been invited
to a Christmas dinner before."

"It is a happy day for us all,"
said the Good Woodsman, smiling at
his friends. "We all have good
things in us and today, Great Wolf
has had the opportunity to show us
how really great he is."

When they had finished, Great Wolf thanked the Good Woodsman, and as the others melted back into the forest he bounded away across the ridge, calling back in a long musical howl.

And ever since that time some people
say, if you listen very closely
to the howling of a wolf on
Christmas, you will hear him call,
Noooooooooo-el////////! in memory
of Great Wolf and the Good Woodsman.
And *Noel,* after all, is really
another word for Christmas.